How to Write and Produce Paper Movies

The Official Guide To Paper Moviemaking

WRITTEN BY

JAIDEN FROST

WRITE YOUR STORY. YOUR WAY.

For Tutorials on how to make paper movies:
www.jaidenfrostpresents.com

For assets on creating paper movies, please visit:
Jaidenfrost.shop

Follow me on Social Media everywhere at:
@jaidenfrostpresents

EVERY BOOK SOLD
IS ONE BOOK DONATED

This book was created in support of the "**Spread The Ink**" fund, where one book will be donated for every copy purchased.

It's essential for me to share the art of creating paper movies, as cinematic storytelling has been transformative in my life. By opening the door to others, I hope to empower individuals to express themselves creatively and experience the magic of storytelling firsthand.

Paper movies offer a unique opportunity to democratize cinematic storytelling, removing exclusivity from the hands of studios and making it accessible to all.

Learn more at:
jaidenfrostpresents.com/spreadtheink

TABLE OF CONTENTS

Quick Explanation

What is a paper movie?

A paper movie is a blend of screenplay and novel, with a narrator acting as the director, using cinematic photographs or illustrations to tell the story.

The narrator is the director.

Paper movies may be written and directed by the same writer, but they don't have to be. While the writer tells you what is happening, the director's voice comes through separately as an omnipotent narrator, giving personal context to the scene, characters, and story.

It's not a paper movie without images.

Accompanied by visual imagery, such as photographs or illustrations, paper movies offer readers a dynamic and imaginative journey into the world of cinematic storytelling.

Without them, it is just a script.

CHAPTER 1

What is a Paper Movie?

Welcome to the world of paper movies, where storytelling meets cinematic imagery to create a truly immersive reading experience.

A paper movie is a unique storytelling format that blends elements of traditional screenplays with the narrative style of a novel and cinematic images.

If a screenplay is a movie's blueprint for the screen, a paper movie is the screen on the page.

Similar to a screenplay, a paper movie presents scenes in a structured format, detailing the action, dialogue, and direction in a present-tense narrative, carefully crafted to set the scene, stating the location, time of day, and key elements that drive the story forward.

What sets paper movies apart is their use of prose reminiscent of a third-person novel. In this narrative approach, the narrator assumes the role of the director, guiding readers through the story with vivid descriptions and insights into the characters' thoughts and emotions. This creates a more immersive reading experience, allowing readers to visualize the story unfolding before their eyes.

This style of writing is called "third-person present-tense omniscient."

In simple terms, when a story is told in the third person, it means the narrator talks about the characters as "he," "she," "they," or "it." Present tense means the story is happening right now, using verbs like "runs" or "jumps."

Now, "omniscient" might sound fancy, but it simply means the narrator knows everything that's going on. It's like the director is a super observer who sees and knows everything, almost like they're a god telling the story.

Like a motion picture, the still pictures need the same presentation. With each scene accompanied by cinematic imagery, such as photographs or illustrations, key moments in the story are brought to life with visuals that enhance the reading experience. These images capture the essence of the scene, providing readers with a deeper understanding of the story and its characters.

One of the most exciting aspects of paper movies, as opposed to normal books, is their unique approach to pacing.

Just like a movie, the length of time it takes to read a paper movie mirrors the pacing of a cinematic experience. With every two pages equating to about one minute of read-time, readers can immerse themselves in the story at a pace that feels familiar and engaging.

So, let's get to it.

Why movies as books?

But you're probably wondering why.
Why not a traditional novel or a movie?

Well, hold onto your bloomers, old-timey snarky-reader from 1906.

What makes a paper movie isn't just how the author writes the story; it is the experience it creates for the reader.

Before we begin our assessment of this question, let's start with numbers.

In 2022, assisted in a survey about whether the book was better than the movie. Of the 10,000+ people we surveyed, 48.43% of adults said they had read an entire book in the past 12 months.

But shockingly, a staggering 87% of them said that overall, they do not "have time to read" and consider most books to be "too long" or "too much of a commitment." And 67% of those who were interviewed said they *preferred reading* books over movies.

Interestingly enough, when it came to having read the books that movies are based on, 34% enjoyed the book, compared to 66% who preferred the film, with 95% citing their "attention span" as the reason for preferring the movie.

Regarding valuing the book beforehand, 34% said they postponed watching a television show or movie to read the book it was based on first.

This aligned with my personal experience as well. Working in the film industry, I would always hear from people that they preferred the intimacy of reading the book over the movie but also felt that movies were just easier to follow.

And there came the final inspiration for a paper movie.

How did this come about?

In 2009, I made a short film in which I had to act. And my acting was so poor that it destroyed the entire picture. The worst part is that I didn't realize until it went viral. I was mocked, ridiculed, and even memed.

But as Dalton Trumbo said, "If it's terrible, there is still a good story in there somewhere." So, I took the images created for the film and tried to do a comic book version. While I preferred it, no one had any interest in it.

Over the next decade, I returned to this style once more. Refining it and tweaking it. But never truly giving it the proper attention. I would go on to ghostwrite for Hollywood, doing television shows, music videos, and movies. Every time I took a step closer to my dream, the more I began to loathe it. I hated the lack of creativity by the producers and the massive egos of the directors.

My dream couldn't come true because it didn't exist.

And then I returned to the paper movie. I injured myself pretty intensely on set and wasn't able to walk for a couple of months, and my anxiety set in. "What if this is my life now, and I can no longer be on set?"

So, I worked meticulously on this idea. Taking the screen to the page. Eventually, I'd recover physically, but the abuse I went through by studios and directors was so intense I was no longer the same person. I was riddled with anxiety that every text was going to be me getting reamed by a director. Every meeting I would have with someone would spiral the moment I spoke my mind. Or even worse, *that every creative idea I would ever have wouldn't ever be allowed to be mine.*

So, I stepped away from Hollywood.

The first paper movie.

It took me a while to produce a paper movie. I was scared it wasn't going to work. After nearly fifteen years of working on something, there was no way I could accept defeat on it. It seemed like with each passing day, it just became more and more difficult to imagine it failing. But my wife finally forced me to take that next step. At that time, the metal band Cultus Black was interested in collaborating with me on their next music video. So I did what I was afraid to do, and I took that plunge with them in the driver's seat as the stars.

And it worked.

Without a chance of argument, it was the best thing I ever did. The reception for *"Cult of Carnival"* was overwhelming. Across all platforms, there were over 1,000 units sold, a staggering 100,000 readers digitally, and a remarkable 75% approval rating.

And though I was nervous about how people were going to receive the format, I couldn't have been more wrong with my anxiety. 83% of our readers said it felt like they had experienced a movie, and 65% said they returned for a second reading after completing it, which is unheard of for a traditional novel.

So I'll be the first to say it.

When it comes to the Paper Movie, the book isn't better than the movie; the book *is* the movie.

So, let's get to work teaching you how to make these wonderful things.

CHAPTER 2

Page Structure

Following the page format is crucial because it helps you estimate how long it will take readers to go through each page. This is where books have always struggled, and cinema has shined. So, it's important to understand how to craft a paper movie in format.

That means it's roughly one minute of reading time for every two pages. The font style and size were chosen to determine read-time and make reading easy, especially for those who may struggle with reading. **Libre Baskerville** is a font known for being reader-friendly for non-readers and is the perfect size and shape for read-time estimation.

This is also why a neurodivergent warning is placed at the beginning of the book to tell readers to look at the scene headings.

Scene headings play a key role in helping readers understand when and where each scene takes place. They provide important information about the time and location, helping the audience grasp the context of the scene.

It's important to note that while this format is a common layout for paper movies, creators have the freedom to personalize their paper movies according to their own preferences and creative ideas.

Page Format

1. **Page Size**: The standard size of a paper movie is 6x9 inches.

2. **Font Choice:** The standard font for paper movies is *Libre Baskerville* in *12-point font.*

3. **Margins**: The *Left Margin* is set at 1.00 inches, and the *Right Margin* is set at 3.50 inches.

4. **New Chapters and Scenes**: New chapters and scenes always begin on the right-hand page. Each new chapter begins with a new scene heading. *Chapters are not named.*

5. **Chapter Headings**: Chapter numbers are presented above the scene image in *bold font at 24-point in size* at the start of a chapter.

6. **Scene Heading**: *The scene heading is written in italics in 10-point font and is center-aligned. The scene location is listed*

at the top, followed by the scene time with a double // before the time.

7. **Action**: Action descriptions are written in 12-point font.

8. **Direction**: Direction is written after the action and is stylized in *italics*.

9. **Character Introduction**: The first time a character is mentioned in the action, their name is written in **bold**.

10. **Dialogue Formatting**: Characters and dialogue are .50 inches indented. Character names are listed first in **bold**, followed by a colon. Parentheticals, if used, follow the character name in italics and 12-point font.

11. **Parentheticals**: Parentheticals are written in italics, enclosed in parentheses, and follow the character's names.

12. **Dialogue**: Dialogue is presented in "quotation marks," following a character tag

13. **Sounds**: Sounds are right-aligned, **bold**, and in *italics*.

14. **Still Images:** Still images are included in an aspect ratio commonly used in cinema or television. The specific aspect ratio is the creative choice of the director.

Through the next five chapters, we will break down each part of the format.

CHAPTER 3

Paper Movie Formatting

Before delving into the intricate details of creating paper movies, it's crucial to grasp the importance of page format. How your paper movie is structured on the page significantly impacts your audience's readability and overall experience. This chapter is designed to break down each section of the page format in easy-to-understand terms, ensuring that you have the knowledge and tools necessary to craft compelling paper movies.

From scene headings to dialogue formatting, every page layout aspect plays a vital role in immersing readers in your cinematic narrative.

Chapter Headings

Chapter Headings begin new chapters and are at the very top of the page. New chapters always begin on the right page. Usually, in paper movies, there are 12 or fewer chapters, but that is the discretion of the director.

Note: Chapters are never named.

Note: Chapters headings are stylized in all caps and bold.

CHAPTER

A SMALL DARK ROOM
// MORNING

Darkness engulfs everything in the hollow black abyss. The light from the outside hallway breaks through the darkness from the edges of the doorway.

Though we can't see her... she's there.

SAVANNAH: (*pleading*) "I'm sorry, Allison. Please don't do what I think you're going to do."

CREEEEEAK...

Scene Headings

When you start a new scene, the location will be in bold, and all caps will be at the top of the page. The time the scene happens will be at the end, after two dashes "//."

The scene heading is Libre Baskerville, at 10-point size, *italics* and **bold**.

For example:

OLD HOUSE // KITCHEN

If more details are needed, like whose house it is or the specific time, they're separated by a colon.

For example:

ANTHONY'S OLD HOUSE: KITCHEN // MORNING

If the heading is too long, the time goes on the next line. Headings shouldn't be

longer than two lines, but if they are, list
them as such.

For example:

ANTHONY'S OLD HOUSE:
GUEST ROOM'S KITCHEN
// MORNING

Note: Scene headings absolutely can not be longer than three lines.

Note: When the SCENE changes, a new page starts with the LOCATION at the top.

Note: If the LOCATION changes within the same SCENE, it doesn't start a new page.

CHAPTER

A SMALL DARK ROOM // MORNING

Darkness engulfs everything in the hollow black abyss. The light from the outside hallway breaks through the darkness from the edges of the doorway.

Though we can't see her... she's there.

SAVANNAH: (*pleading*) "I'm sorry, Allison. Please don't do what I think you're going to do."

CREEEEEAK.

Action

Written in the third person-present tense, this is the story's main narrative from an omnipotent perspective. This creates visual exposition for the audience, giving insight into the story unfolding and its characters.

Action doesn't always feature the action. Sometimes, it deviates from the action and gives a backstory. Or how the character feels or what they're thinking. The action is an omnipotent camera capable of reading thoughts and showing the past.

Note: If the action is written in the present tense, it has to be reflected with a scene change.

Note: The backstory is always paraphrased and written in the third person.

CHAPTER

A SMALL DARK ROOM
// MORNING

Darkness engulfs everything in the hollow black abyss. The light from the outside hallway breaks through the darkness from the edges of the doorway.

Though we can't see her... she's there.

SAVANNAH: (*pleading*) "I'm sorry, Allison. Please don't do what I think you're going to do."

CREEEEEAK.

Backstory

As I stated in "Action," when a Backstory is read, it should only be written in *past tense*. Backstories will present themselves at random times at the writer's and director's will. This can give context to a character's decision or emotion or simply inform the audience of something that doesn't warrant a flashback scene change.

The following page is an excerpt from "Cult of Carnival."

Note: Backstories can go on for as long as you want. This is the perk of paper movies. Use discretion, but always remember the choice is yours.

Illuminated by the fiery flicker of a small torch, Harker hunches over her makeup desk in the corner of the tent.

There was no reason to be here anymore, but she didn't know what else to do.

Harker would frequently be hazed by others in the show for the time spent on her character's look. Because to them, no matter how much she was family, she wasn't actually part of the *show*. She wasn't a performer, had no talents, and wasn't even featured in the promotional fliers.

She was just a barker.

Direction

Direction is a short one-to-two-line statement made from the author's point of view on the situation unfolding in the story. While the action is stylized as an informative narrative, the direction is very specific to the director and can be written informally if the director decides, as if the author stopped reading the story to talk candidly to the audience.

Their job is to direct the audience's perspective of a scene or situation. No matter what.

Note: Think of it as God speaking directly to the audience with their opinion.

Note: The director can be untrustworthy, judgemental, or however they want to present.

CHAPTER

A SMALL DARK ROOM
// MORNING

Darkness engulfs everything in the hollow black abyss. The light from the outside hallway breaks through the darkness from the edges of the doorway.

Though we can't see her... she's there.

SAVANNAH: (*pleading*) "I'm sorry, Allison. Please don't do what I think you're going to do."

CREEEEEAK.

Character Tag

When a character speaks, their name is always capitalized and bold when listed before their dialogue.

Separating the dialogue allows the audience to focus purely on the words being spoken by the character. This is what gives a "script-like" presentation to a paper movie but also increases the readability. The audience can go back and forth between the pages and quickly depict what is being said. So, in the case that they stop mid-chapter or scene, all it takes is a quick browse, and then they're caught up. Similar to rewinding a movie.

Note: Sometimes, characters don't have real names. They can be "RANDOM MAN" until that character's name is revealed.

CHAPTER

A SMALL DARK ROOM
// MORNING

Darkness engulfs everything in the hollow black abyss. The light from the outside hallway breaks through the darkness from the edges of the doorway.

Though we can't see her... she's there.

SAVANNAH: (*pleading*) "I'm sorry, Allison. Please don't do what I think you're going to do."

CREEEEEAK.

Parenthetical

A parenthetical is a traditional playwriting technique that gives information on how the character delivers a line of dialogue. They are listed next to the character tag for easy readability.

When actors collaborate with you, they may change these tags in order to convey the way they would have performed these lines.

Note: Never have the parenthetical extend to a second line. Keep them concise.

Note: Action can be featured, but keep it short.

Note: Screenwriters, never use (beat) to break up dialogue. This holds no relevance to the readers. Pauses must be conveyed in action.

CHAPTER

A SMALL DARK ROOM
// MORNING

Darkness engulfs everything in the hollow black abyss. The light from the outside hallway breaks through the darkness from the edges of the doorway.

Though we can't see her... she's there.

SAVANNAH: *(pleading)* "I'm sorry, Allison. Please don't do what I think you're going to do."

CREEEEEAK.

Dialogue

The dialogue is any time a character is heard speaking. If the dialogue is spoken aloud, it is presented in the *dialogue format*. Whether in communication with other characters or with themselves.

Dialogue should **ALWAYS** be written the way it would be said. While grammar matters, it is less relevant here.

Note: Every character should have a distinct voice. Try experimenting with phonic pronunciations and giving characters accents.

CHAPTER

A SMALL DARK ROOM
// MORNING

Darkness engulfs everything in the hollow black abyss. The light from the outside hallway breaks through the darkness from the edges of the doorway.

Though we can't see her... she's there.

SAVANNAH: (*pleading*) "I'm sorry, Allison. Please don't do what I think you're going to do."

CREEEEEAK.

Sound Ques

When incorporating sound cues into your paper movie, it's essential to consider their narrative significance. Sound cues that serve a specific narrative purpose will be highlighted for emphasis. These cues are italicized and bold, drawing attention to their importance, and are positioned on the right side of the page for clarity.

Note: Not all sounds warrant this special formatting. The writer exercises discretion in determining which sounds merit the use of sound cues, ensuring that only those with narrative relevance are highlighted in this manner.

Note: Sounds are always "sounded out" and form onamonapias.

CHAPTER

A SMALL DARK ROOM
// MORNING

Darkness engulfs everything in the hollow black abyss. The light from the outside hallway breaks through the darkness from the edges of the doorway.

Though we can't see her... she's there.

SAVANNAH: (*pleading*) "I'm sorry, Allison. Please don't do what I think you're going to do."

CREEEEEAK...

IN FINAL...

Write your movie the way you want it.
Despite the guidelines in how it is
formatted, you are in control of how you
write your paper movie.

Now that you have learned how to write
one let's discuss the arc flow of a
cinematic story.

CHAPTER 4

Arc Flow

In the realm of paper movies, the arc flow serves as the guiding path that a story follows, determining its beginning, middle, and end. Similar to the peaks and valleys of a roller coaster ride, a paper movie's arc should feature moments of tension and release, with rises and falls in the narrative momentum. These fluctuations are determined by the plot phases, each offering five potential options ranging from *very good to very bad.*

By assessing the arc tension of each plot phase, creators gain insight into the trajectory of their main character's journey throughout the story. This understanding not only shapes the development of the protagonist but also aids in crafting a cohesive and satisfying conclusion to the narrative.

When writing paper movies, each chapter is often thematically aligned with one of the plot phases, although directors retain the flexibility to deviate from this structure if desired.

Additionally, creators have the option to select from four pre-made Arc Flows:

Successful Ending, Successful Failure, Failure Ending, and Failing Success.

Alternatively, they can tailor their own arc flow using the provided chart, allowing for a personalized and dynamic storytelling experience.

Note: You're welcome to skip this part. These are meant to guide, not control. It's ultimately your movie.

TENSION	DESCRIPTION
VERY GOOD	The absolute best outcome.
GOOD	A decent but less-than-perfect outcome.
NEUTRAL	Not a great outcome, but not a bad outcome.
BAD	An awful, but less than the terrible outcome.
VERY BAD	The absolute worst outcome.

Successful Ending

The primary conflict is resolved as the protagonist achieves their desire and needs.

Chapter 1	*Neutral*
Chapter 2	*Neutral*
Chapter 3	*Neutral*
Chapter 4	*Good*
Chapter 5	*Bad*
Chapter 6	*Bad*
Chapter 7	*Neutral*
Chapter 8	*Good*
Chapter 9	*Neutral*
Chapter 10	*Very Bad*
Chapter 11	*Very Good*
Chapter 12	*Very Good*

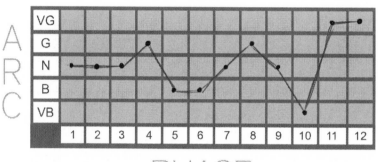

ARC

PHASE

51

Failure Ending

The protagonist ultimately fails to achieve their desire and need, and the antagonist prevails.

Chapter 1	*Neutral*
Chapter 2	*Neutral*
Chapter 3	*Neutral*
Chapter 4	*Good*
Chapter 5	*Neutral*
Chapter 6	*Bad*
Chapter 7	*Neutral*
Chapter 8	*Good*
Chapter 9	*Good*
Chapter 10	*Very Good*
Chapter 11	*Very Bad*
Chapter 12	*Very Bad*

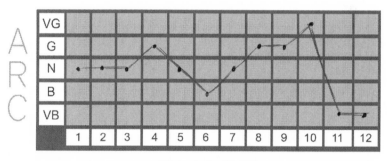

Failing Success

The protagonist fails to achieve their desire but ultimately succeeds in achieving their need.

Chapter 1	*Bad*
Chapter 2	*Bad*
Chapter 3	*Neutral*
Chapter 4	*Good*
Chapter 5	*Bad*
Chapter 6	*Very Bad*
Chapter 7	*Neutral*
Chapter 8	*Good*
Chapter 9	*Good*
Chapter 10	*Very Good*
Chapter 11	*Neutral*
Chapter 12	*Bad*

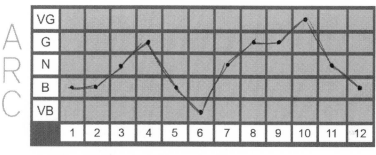

Successful Failure

The protagonist succeeds in achieving their desire but ultimately fails in achieving their need.

Chapter 1	*Good*
Chapter 2	*Good*
Chapter 3	*Neutral*
Chapter 4	*Very Good*
Chapter 5	*Neutral*
Chapter 6	*Bad*
Chapter 7	*Neutral*
Chapter 8	*Good*
Chapter 9	*Neutral*
Chapter 10	*Very Bad*
Chapter 11	*Neutral*
Chapter 12	*Good*

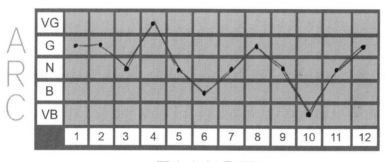

CHAPTER 5

The Plot Phases

In the art of paper movies, a plot phase serves as a fundamental unit of plot progression. These phases represent pivotal moments in the narrative that drive the story forward.

Unlike scene changes, plot phases may not be overtly discernible to the audience; rather, they serve as guiding markers for the writer throughout the storytelling process. As you craft your paper movie, it's essential to consult your arc flow, as each phase may yield a distinct feel or outcome based on the trajectory of your story.

While there is no strict maximum or minimum limit to the number of scenes within each phase, it's important to remember the cinematic nature of the medium. Pacing is important in maintaining audience engagement and cinematic momentum.

Note: Just because it needs to be said doesn't mean it needs to be read.

Prologue

The prologue serves as a captivating introduction to the paper movie, crafted from the perspective of the director. Unlike other chapters, the prologue doesn't depict any action; instead, it focuses on establishing the mood and tone of the paper movie.

This section is where the director's unique voice and style shine through, captivating the audience from the very beginning and setting the stage for the unfolding narrative.

Chapter 1 Arc

This is the audience's first impression of the character they will follow, almost like a handshake introduction with a stranger.

Chapter 1 establishes the main character to the audience by allowing them to see them interact with others and the world they are in. Try introducing them through interaction and conversation. Establish their life, what they are capable of, the status quo, and the world in which the story occurs.

The audience may meet the antagonist in this phase, but only briefly, and the conflict has not yet presented itself.

Chapter 2 Arc

Chapter 2 marks the starting point of our narrative journey. Here, we enter a crucial phase where the protagonist gains clarity on their story's central focus or objective.

This phase serves as the catalyst, igniting the primary tension of the narrative and propelling the protagonist forward on their journey. It unfolds after the initial scenes of our paper movie, setting the stage for the unfolding drama and character development that lie ahead.

Chapter 3 Arc

The story must begin. This is when the protagonist can no longer live comfortably in the environment established in *Chapter 1*. This is the moment that catapults them into the story.

This is the chapter where the antagonist presents themselves as the protagonist's foil. At this moment, the antagonist and the protagonist are equally matched in the audience's eyes.

Despite the protagonist not currently possessing the ability to achieve their goal, they have to blindly believe in themselves enough to move forward. They will ultimately push toward the conflict with that confidence but will **undoubtedly be wrong.** *Chapter 3* concludes when the character has learned their *goal* and embarks on their journey to accomplish it.

Chapter 4 Arc

This chapter will be where the protagonists will look as strong (*or as weak*) as they can, but no matter what, the audience must be able to believe in them.

Whether or not the story results in a success or a failure, this moment should be the strongest the protagonist appears in the story, as they will undergo significant changes during this phase to achieve their overall goal.

Chapter 4 concludes when the character learns vital information that ultimately leads them to their *goal*.

Chapter 5 Arc

This is where the antagonist retakes control of the story, foiling the protagonist's progression. At this point, the protagonist should be **incapable** of achieving their goal.

The protagonist has attempted to resolve their problem but has struggled, as they have not acquired the necessary skills or information to accomplish their goal. The antagonist uses this weakness to their advantage and slam the door shut on progression.

Whether the story concludes with success or failure, this is the highest moment for the antagonist. They will not be more villainous than at this moment.

Chapter 6 Arc

This is rock bottom for the protagonist. If they were anyone else, the journey would stop here. But they're not just any character; they're the protagonist. This is when they realize that they have lost everything they have gained. Or that everything they initially wanted has no meaning.

Their attempt wasn't enough whether they succeeded or failed at their goal.

This will be the first time the protagonist will taste success or failure. This moment will mirror the conclusion of the story. If they succeed, this success will be a lighter version of the final phase. If your protagonist fails, this phase will also conclude with a lighter version of their absolute failure.

Chapter 7 Arc

This is the moment where the audience gets to explore the world that they are in. Everything that needs to be established has been established, so this is the time that the audience gets to breathe. To back away from the story's tension or the fast-paced action and just exist.

This can be with a fun montage of events, a deep conversation between two characters, a flashback, a trivial moment of character development, etc. This phase allows the audience to reconnect with the characters and learn more about them. Perhaps who they were or how they've grown since *Chapter 1*.

This phase always ends with the protagonist deciding to move forward in the story.

Chapter 8 Arc

The fastest phase in the movie, as this is primarily filled with action.

It's a brief offensive flurry by the protagonist to accomplish their goal, but ultimately, the antagonist stops their momentum. They would have achieved their goal if the timing and circumstances were right. But alas, they were not capable of doing so.

Whether the story is successful for the protagonist or not, this is always the highest moment for the antagonist.

Chapter 9 Arc

Just as all seemed to be lost, this is the "ah-ha" moment for the protagonist. Every loss they have sustained, every win they have achieved, and every speck of knowledge they have ever acquired all come together and breathe new life into the protagonist.

Before, they could not fulfill their goals, but now, they indeed can. They officially have all the tools needed to accomplish their goal, and now they push forward with the determination to win.

Chapter 10 Arc

This is the point in the paper movie that concludes the protagonist's initial objective before continuing to the actual conclusion. The audience had all right to believe the story was about to conclude, but it does anything but. This is where the notable "twist" happens. Simply put, this is the climax of their goal *as they knew it*.

Just as the characters expect to accomplish their goal, they have again underestimated their foe. And have to rethink their strategy to win. The shift can either be a change to the protagonist's overall perspective or, in more severe cases, the entire goal of the protagonist can change depending on the story's trajectory.

Chapter 10 must remain within the boundaries of possibility for the protagonist. This phase concludes with the central tensions of the story being brought to a climactic conclusion.

Chapter 11 Arc

Everything leads to this moment, and good or bad, every story must come to a close. Even if the audience is disappointed with the outcome, the goal should always be to send them home happy. With a good story, even the most negative endings have a satisfying conclusion. Remember, your antagonist is a part of the story as well. And their success is the protagonist's failure.

Whether the protagonist achieves their goal or fails, they remain changed because of their journey.

Chapter 12 Arc

The paper movie's story has concluded.
This will be the last thing your audience
thinks about as your story comes to a
close. If *Chapter 2* is the catalyst for the
start of the story, *Chapter 12* is the
goodbye. This scene takes us from the
present-tense storytelling and concludes
with the final moments before the
credits.

Epilogue Arc

Unlike the prologue, the epilogue provides closure to the narrative journey. It is written from the perspective of the director, offering final reflections and insights into the story's resolution. While the epilogue doesn't feature action, it serves as a poignant conclusion, wrapping up loose ends and leaving a lasting impression on the audience.

Note: If the paper movie intends to continue into a sequel, this chapter will tease this.

CHAPTER 6

Producing Paper Movies

Welcome to the chapter on producing paper movies. Now that you know how to write one, it's time for us to explore the intricate process of bringing your paper movie to life. We'll delve into the collaborative aspects of working with actors.

Additionally, we'll discuss the art of creating cinematic imagery for your paper movie, immersing readers in visually captivating scenes.

Working With Actors

Actors have a certain amount of control over their characters. They're more than just models. They work with the writer and director to make sure their character is being portrayed the way they would have wanted.

Once the script is finalized, it's then distributed to the actors, who meticulously review their lines, providing insightful notes and suggestions to the writer/director regarding their character.

The following pages will break down the collaborative process of acting in a paper movie. This collaborative method encourages actors to feel a strong connection to the project, fostering a sense of ownership and commitment. It goes beyond simply portraying a character; it requires a significant investment of creativity to breathe life into a character on the page. Therefore, it's essential for actors to feel a sense of ownership over the characters they portray, as it enriches the creative process and enhances the authenticity of their performances.

Rewriting Dialogue

Actors possess a unique understanding of their characters' voices and nuances. This means that actors are vital in giving useful feedback on their characters' dialogue, making sure it is accurate to their perspective of their character. Because the actor's voice isn't being used, the actor should be meticulous in determining *what* and *how* it is said.

Any ideas they have to improve the dialogue are discussed with the writer. Then, it's up to the writer, with input from the director, to decide if the changes should be made. It's a team effort to make sure the dialogue fits perfectly with the character and the story.

Determining Tone

Actors play a pivotal role in establishing the emotional performance of their characters. They determine whether their character's reactions align with the story and suggest changes as necessary. Parentheticals serve as performance cues, offering insights into the tone of dialogue. These indicators, placed before lines in parenthesis, highlight significant tonal shifts. *Remember, they are used sparingly so as to not "over-act".*

> **CHARACTER**: (*tone*) "This is a line of dialogue."

Performing

In paper movies, the story is told through still photographs instead of moving images like in traditional movies. This means they have to express emotions and tell the story using only pictures. Memorizing lines isn't necessary because the focus is on showing emotions through facial expressions and body language rather than speaking the lines.

To help actors understand which moments in the story need to be shown visually, they're given a detailed list called a shot list. This list tells them exactly when and where they need to perform for the camera. By knowing beforehand what images are needed, actors can prepare themselves mentally and emotionally for each scene. They focus solely on creating powerful and emotive still images that capture the essence of their character's emotions and actions.

On-Set Dynamics

During the production phase, directors play a crucial role in guiding actors through their performances. They provide actors with specific instructions and visual cues to ensure that the captured images accurately reflect the scene's moment. Directors also help actors understand the emotional context of each scene. A common technique is using on-set music to enhance the mood.

Additionally, directors communicate their preferences for cinematographic style, such as whether the image will be captured using singular still photographs or capturing the performance in motion and choosing the still later. The chosen cinematography style is indicated in the shot list. This ensures that the actor is prepared for the performance.

Table Reads

While a table read with the entire cast can be beneficial, it's not mandatory. Though not always necessary, they are real-time, in-person feedback opportunities for the cast and crew in regard to the characters being portrayed. During table reads, actors consult their notes or ideas about how they think their characters should behave.

Discuss with your director if a table read will be performed.

Capturing Cinematic Still Frames

The imagery is what finishes the paper movie. It's what gives the imagery that defines the look and feel of a paper movie. Until the cinematic imagery is added, the paper movie is nothing more than a script. The images are what bring the paper movie to life.

They define its look and feel, transforming it from a mere script into a cinematic experience.

Selecting the Frame

The amount of images is always up to you. However, one rule is that every scene should begin with an image. If other images are added throughout the scenes, then that is at the director's discretion. Although, how you want to capture images is entirely up to you. You should always aim for a cinematic presentation. That's what sets this apart from other illustrative books.

A picture speaks a thousand words. So, the frames that are determined for the scenes should depict the exact moments that accurately portray your visual vision for the p/movie. Although you theoretically could fill the page with frames, this wouldn't read very well in the paper movie format. Rather, it would feel more like a comic book or storyboard.

Note: Your images should complement the words, not the other way around.

Framing your Images

The framing of your images should mimic the aspect ratio commonly found in movies (e.g., 16:9, 2.39:1, 4:3, etc).

Position the subjects and objects strategically within the frame, finding unique ways to create a cinematic image.

The Visual Style of Paper Movies

Traditionally, the paper movie visual style was created using live-action imagery, processed and rotoscoped.

Rotoscoping is a technique used in animation where animators trace over live-action frames. This technique allows for a seamless blend of live-action and illustration, offering a unique visual style.

In the early days of Disney feature films, rotoscoping played a crucial role in bringing characters to life on the screen. Walt Disney and his team utilized rotoscoping to capture the intricate movements and expressions of human characters in films such as "Snow White and the Seven Dwarfs" and "Cinderella." By tracing over live-action footage of actors performing specific movements or actions, animators were able to achieve a level of realism and detail that was unprecedented in animated films at the time. This innovative approach helped establish Disney as a pioneer in the world of animation and set a new standard for the industry.

That's why this visual choice was determined to be the staple of the paper movie genre. By taking live-action photographs of actors and converting them into illustrations, the images take life in a new form. When marketing a paper movie, the style isn't confused with anything else. Be it motion pictures, standard photography, or comic books. Paper movies have their own defined look.

Also, this style allows actors to visually portray their characters, adding to the overall cinematic experience.

Note: While this is the LOOK of paper movies, nothing is stopping you from creating your look with anything else.

For those who are interested in doing this style, check *jaidenfrost.shop* **for any assets or tutorials.**

Determining Color for Your Paper Movies

When it comes to making paper movies, one of the crucial decisions is determining the color palette for your images. Traditionally, paper movies have a different presentation when in print or digital.

Printed paper movies are usually printed in black and white, a price-conscious choice but also a choice deeply rooted in the history of cinema. Back in the early days of film, audiences often associated black-and-white movies with a sense of sophistication and higher quality. This perception stemmed from the notion that black-and-white imagery allowed for a greater focus on storytelling and character development. This was a win/win for studios because it allowed production companies to produce movies much cheaper without sacrificing the perspective of quality.

Readers are no different and usually prefer black-and-white printed imagery in their books, as opposed to full color.

This gives paper movies a chance to print cheaper while offering a stylistic nod to the traditional aesthetic of classic cinema.

However, with the rise of digital distribution channels, paper movies have also embraced the beauty of full color. When images are distributed digitally, either through marketing, e-books, or video, they take on a more "streaming" presentation, featuring full spectrum colors, sharp details, and a deeper dynamic range.

Note: Despite the transition to digital, the imagery still retains an "organic" quality, reminiscent of a printed picture. This blend of traditional aesthetics and modern technology allows paper movies to adapt to changing audience preferences while maintaining their distinctive charm and appeal.

CHAPTER 7

Go Make Yours!

And that's it! Now, you have all of the tools to write and produce your own paper movies. When I initially came up with this format, I never expected it to take off the way it has.

But I'm glad I did.

As I said in the opening chapters of this book, I'm always looking for new paper movies to produce and distribute. If you've written one, please visit jaidenfrostpresents.com/submit to submit yours.

I am also always looking for paper movie writers, actors, and photographers. If you're interested in pursuing a career in the paper pictures, please go to jaidenfrostpresents.com/audition

When I created this format, I didn't realize how much it was going to become my passion. It has literately become my favorite genre of storytelling. So whether it's mine or someone else's, I'm excited to read them. So, even if you just want me to read yours, please feel free to reach out to me. I'm as much of a fan as I am a creator. So, let's build this industry, one picture at a time.

Welcome to Hollybook.
You're gonna be a star.